First published as *Vuur en vlam* by publishing house Manteau, part of WPG Publishers Belgium, in 2012. Published by agreement with WPG Publishers Belgium.

Sky Pony Press books may be purchased in bulk at special discounts for sales promotion, corporate gifts, fund-raising, or educational purposes. Special editions can also be created to specifications. For details, contact the Special Sales Dèpartment, Sky Pony Press, 307 West 36th Street, 11th Floor, New York, NY 10018 or info@skyhorsepublishing.com.

Sky Pony® is a registered trademark of Skyhorse Publishing, Inc.®, a Delaware corporation.

Visit our website at www.skyponypress.com.

10 9 8 7 6 5 4 3 2 1

Manufactured in China, November 2014
This product conforms to CPSIA 2008

Library of Congress Cataloging-in-Publication Data is available on file.

Cover design by Pigmalion vzw
Cover illustration credit Tineke Van Hemeldonck

Print ISBN: 978-1-63220-599-5
Ebook ISBN: 978-1-63220-835-4

Dragon Fire

A Story about Family and Cancer

Written by Geert De Kockere and An Dom
Illustrated by Tineke Van Hemeldonck

Translated by Thomas W. Mertens

Sky Pony Press
New York

It's summer, and it's hot. The sun spits fire like a giant dragon.
Mr. and Mrs. Dragon love the summer.
And they love fire. Fire and flames.
"Fire is life, and life is fire!" they often say.
Their dragon children also love fire.
They, too, are often ablaze with fire and flames,
especially when they play. The glowing makes them grow.

At night, when it gets dark, Mr. and Mrs. Dragon and the Dragon children
stand side by side and breathe fire together.
The one who breathes fire the farthest wins!
It sparks and twinkles; it blazes and flares.
It's a true fireworks show. Fire and flames! They're so strong!

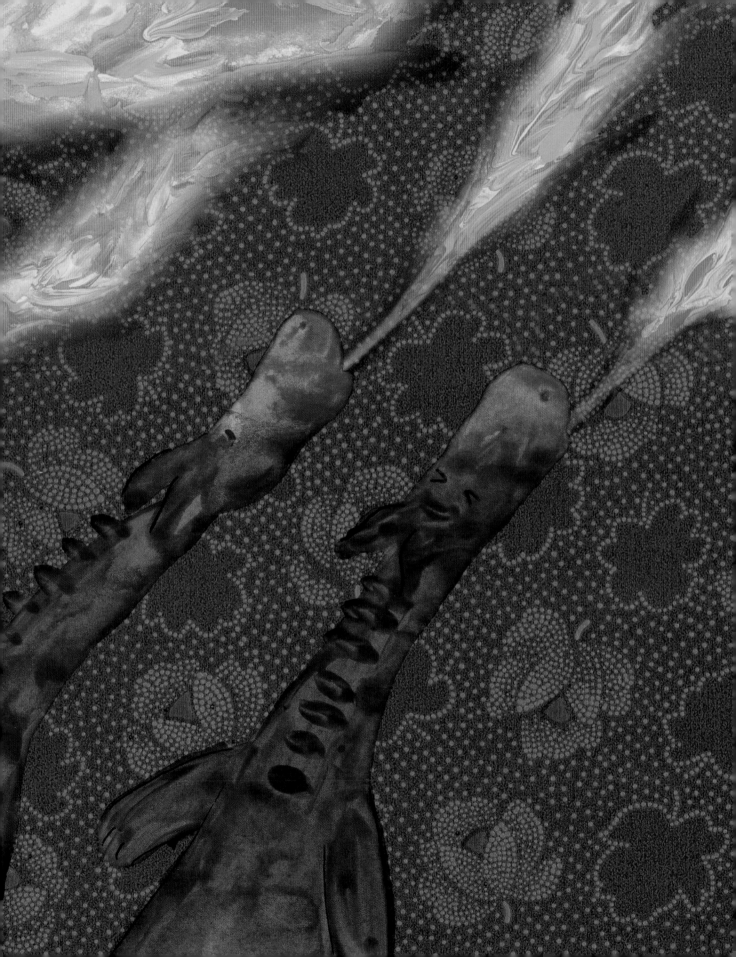

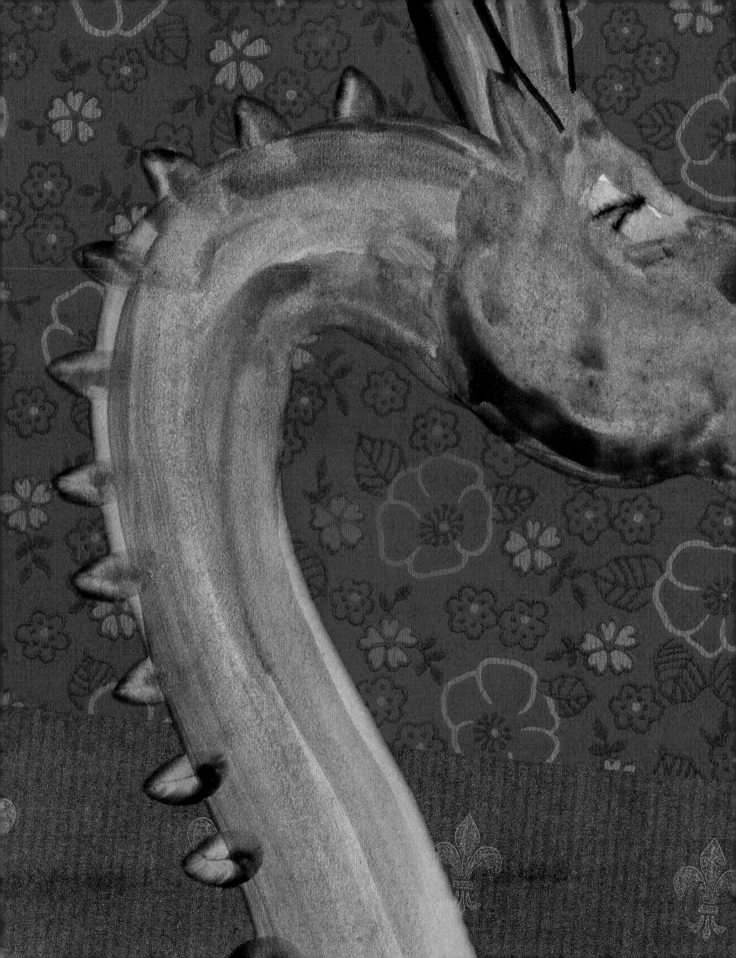

But one night, Mrs. Dragon can't breathe fire anymore.
Not a flame. There's nothing but a puff of smoke.
"Oh well," Mrs. Dragon says. "Tomorrow, I'll breathe fire again, and flames.
Farther than ever. You'll see."
But the next day, she still can't breathe fire. Or the night after that.
"There's something in your belly," the dragon doctor says. "Something bad.
It puts out your fire. I'll give you something for it. It's yucky, but it helps.
If we're lucky, you'll have your fire and flames back."

Mrs. Dragon is feeling bad. "I want my fire back!" she says.
She curls up in her nest, for weeks on end. She's so tired.
She misses her flames. *Fire is life, and life is fire,* she thinks.
Mr. Dragon and the Dragon children help wherever they can.
With the yucky medicine. And with each other. It's not easy for them.

But look! Winter's over, and Mrs. Dragon comes out of her nest more often. There's even a small fire again. "A baby flame!" the children laugh.

"You know what?" says Mr. Dragon, because he's happy, too.

"Let's go to Dragon Island! I think we deserve it!"

"And when summer comes around, we'll all breathe fire again!" the Dragon children say. "Whoever breathes fire the farthest wins! Okay? Okay, Mom?"

Or not?
Summer is still a long time away when
Mrs. Dragon can barely come out of her nest.
Her dragon head looks sad; her dragon body is weak.
"The bad thing is back," the dragon doctor says.
"This time it's everywhere. It's eating your body. I'll give
you something really powerful," he says.
"Maybe. Just maybe. Who knows . . ." He doesn't say anything more.

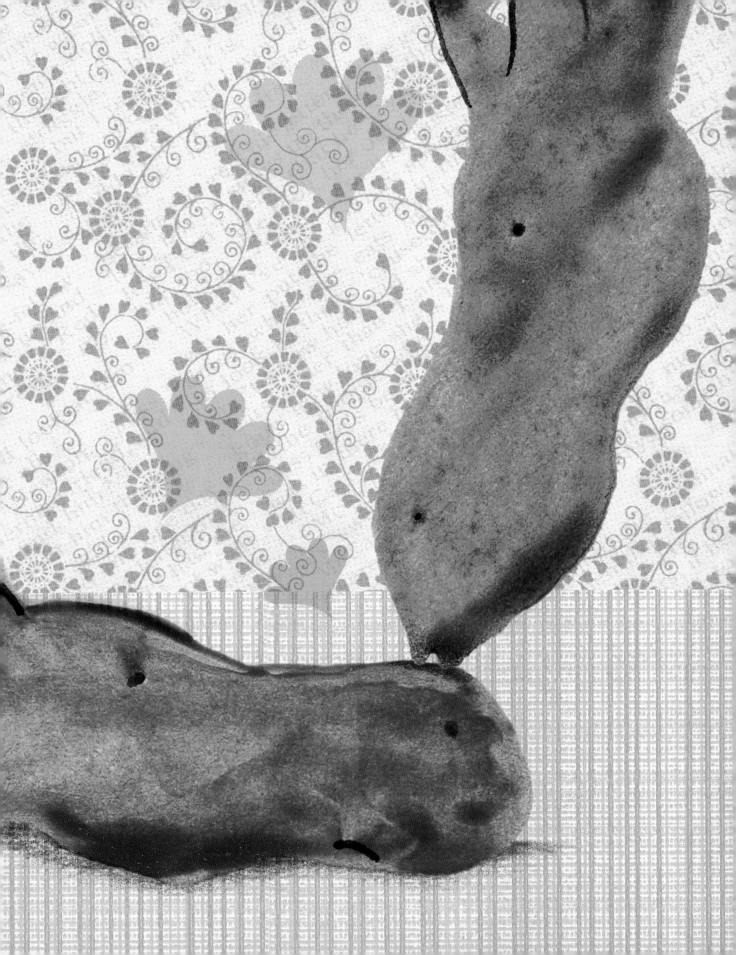

The fire inside Mrs. Dragon goes out almost completely.
And without fire, there's not much she can do.
Giving a hug is still possible. And a kiss, too.
At least that's something. Who knows . . .
Mr. Dragon and the Dragon children feel bad.
But they don't give up.
They keep on hugging; they keep on kissing.
They don't breathe fire anymore.
Not without Mrs. Dragon.

Why? Mrs. Dragon wonders. *Where is my fire? Where is my flame?*
She gets smaller and thinner. Her body is so tired. It's not shiny anymore.
Not even with all the hugs and kisses she gets.
Sometimes there's some fire. Just for a moment. And then everyone is happy.
Mr. Dragon, Mrs. Dragon, and the Dragon children, as happy as they can be,
for just a moment.

"I can't go on anymore," Mrs. Dragon says one night.
And she looks at the sky. There are stars. They're shining bright.
There is still fire there, she thinks. *There still is life.*
"I can't . . ." Mrs. Dragon says.
"I understand," says Mr. Dragon. He chokes up.
"Sleep tight," the Dragon children say. "Sleep tight . . ."
They give her one last hug, one very last kiss.
And then the fire goes out. Completely . . .

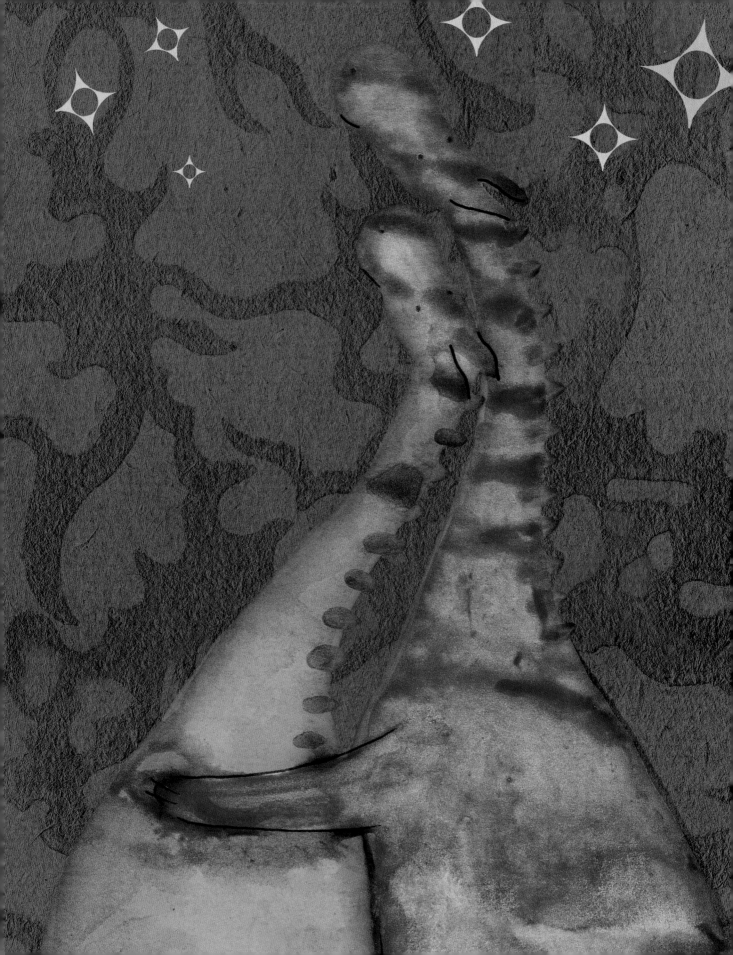

Mrs. Dragon is gone. And yet she's not.
Because Mr. Dragon and the Dragon children still see her every day.
As often as they want. As beautifully as they can remember. Somewhere deep inside.
They can still feel the hugs, and they still give the kisses.
And maybe, they bravely think, *maybe someday we'll breathe fire together again!*
Maybe . . . but they don't know exactly. Or when. Or how. Or how many times.

It's summer again. Mr. Dragon and the Dragon children
are standing outside in the dark.
"Should we breathe fire again?" Mr. Dragon asks
quietly.
"Alright," the Dragon children say. "For a little
while . . ."
And so they do.
Not to see who can do it the farthest. No, not to do
it the farthest.
They try doing it as beautifully as they can.
Yes, as beautifully as they can.

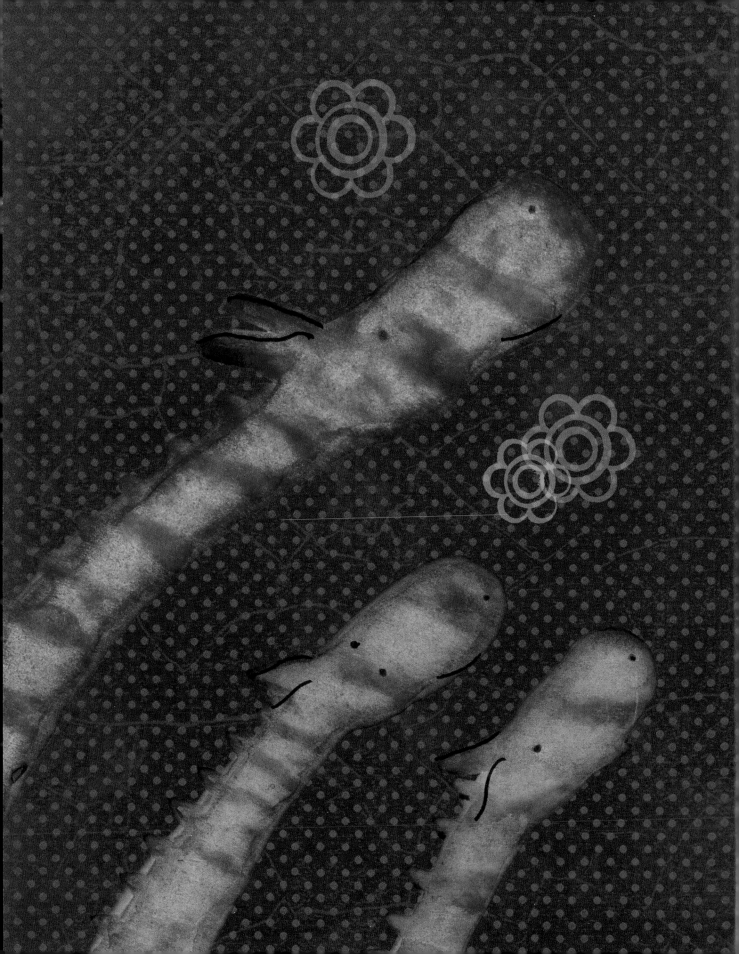

And then something special happens. High in the sky, between the sparkling stars, a flame shoots through the dark.
"Mom!" the Dragon children shout. "That was Mom! Did you see that? That was so beautiful!"
"Yes!" Mr. Dragon shouts. "So beautiful that Mom wins this time."
And all three of them nod.
"Again tomorrow?" Mr. Dragon asks.
"Again tomorrow," the Dragon children answer.
"To see who can do it the most beautiful . . ."
"Yes, the most beautiful . . ." Mr. Dragon says.
There's fire and flames again . . .

In May 2010, I found out I had breast cancer. I had no choice but to fight. It became a war of attrition, both mentally and physically. The chemotherapy made me so sick I often wondered if it was all worth it. The mental anguish was the worst of all. How do you tell your children that Mom has a life threatening illness? How do you deal with the idea that you might die?

I survived those months with the love and support of my family. I was cut off from living life, however. Then I decided to write a book about cancer, together with my sister Ilse. Not a corny story, but one in which the love between parent and child is so strong, it transcends the boundary of life and death. I translated the belief that there is "something" after the death into the hopeful ending of the story.

In the beginning of 2011, the treatments were finished. I felt I was growing stronger with each passing month, and I was optimistic about the future. At the beginning of July, however, came the second crushing blow: relapse! This time, it had spread to the bones and lungs. Halfway through September, treatment was halted. It had spread to the brain . . . This was the end.

The oncologists, Professor Altintas and Professor Huizing, had done everything they could. I want to thank them both from the bottom of my heart for their warm and kind care, and for their sincere emotional involvement. I also want to express my thanks to my dear friends, colleagues, neighbors, members of my extended family, and the nursing staff. I am amazed by so much heartfelt friendship!